0 026 460 20X 62

KT-387-797

UDDY BOGEY
The Ogre Yogi

For Ian Dicks
J. W.

For the Loupas Family, Klub Barbounia members
K. P.

ORCHARD BOOKS
96 Leonard Street, London EC2A 4XD
Orchard Books Australia
32/45-51 Huntley Street, Alexandria, NSW 2015
ISBN 978 1 84362 160 7 (paperback)
First published in Great Britain in 2004
First paperback publication in 2005
Text © Jeanne Willis 2004
Illustrations © Korky Paul 2004
The rights of Jeanne Willis to be identified as the author
and of Korky Paul to be identified as the illustrator of this
work have been asserted by them in accordance with the
Copyright, Designs and Patents Act, 1988.
A CIP catalogue record for this book is available
from the British Library.
3 5 7 9 10 8 6 4 (paperback)
Printed in Great Britain

IDDY BOGEY
The Ogre Yogi

SEFTON LIBRARY SERVICES	
002646020	
Bertrams	26/08/2009
JFic	
Mari	£3.99

Jeanne Willis * Korky Paul

ORCHARD BOOKS

IDDY BOGEY
The Ogre Yogi

Greetings, Un-enlightened One!
Your face is reddened by the sun.
Or is it that you blush to be
So close to one as wise as me?

Rest a while! Relax and stop
Upon this sacred mountain top
With Iddy Bogey - for I speak
True wisdom, which I know you seek.

For I am he, the Yogi Ogre,
Meditating in my toga.
And my task is very plain –
To tackle stress and mental strain.

I help the creatures folk avoid.
The Yeti? He was paranoid.
He thought nobody liked him, see?
And came along for therapy.

A yoga course to make him calm
Improved his posture and his charm.
And tied up in a hairy knot,
His confidence increased a lot.

I offered him a cleansing grape
And helped him find his Inner-Ape
With hypnotherapy and sound,
And massaging his head around.

It did the trick and in the end
I heard he found himself a friend.
He learnt to dance and sing and joke
Instead of terrifying folk.

Some patients tell me in a session
That they suffer from depression.
And here I humbly must confess
I've had all manner of success.

I have even helped The Reaper.
He was Grim - an awful sleeper!
He would lie awake for hours
Obsessed with funerals and flowers.

The problem seemed so black and white
That Colour Therapy was right.
I swopped his gloomy, grey kagoul
For something cheerful, young and cool.

I stuck a pom-pom on his sickle,
Telling him to go and tickle
Folk, and show the funny side
Of death. They laughed until they died!

The hardest case I ever had
Came to me from Jalalabad
By carpet in a puff of smoke.
"Give up fags!" I said. "You'll choke."

The genie (for that's who he was)
Had come to visit me because
He couldn't get into his lamp
For claustrophobia and cramp.

"It's far too small inside!" he said.
"I stub my toes and bang my head.
It makes me ill! If I go back
I'll have a panicky attack."

"It makes my turban throb," he cried,
"And I get butterflies inside.
It makes my head and fingers jerk
And granting wishes doesn't work!"

He then explained at weary length
The phobia had sapped his strength,
And if his master summoned him
The chances of a wish were slim.

If, for example, he expressed
A wish to be more richly dressed,
The wish backfired and he would stand
Stark naked in the desert sand.

Or say his master wished for snow -
Instead, a howling storm would blow,
With camels falling from the sky.
"How odd!" I said. "I wonder why?"

I checked his pulse and racing heart
And asked, "When did the trouble start?"
And, Is it possible to tell
If lamps were worst, or jars as well?

And if he tried a bigger bottle
Would he feel his larynx throttle?
And was 'size' the real issue?
(Here, I handed him a tissue.)

"I don't know," the genie wept.
"In all the vessels I've been kept
This is the nastiest of all.
I'm telling you, it is far too small."

I found a tape and this I placed
Around his rather tubby waist,
Announcing, as I felt I ought,
"The lamp is not the thing at fault!"

"You are too big, Sir, it is clear,
To squeeze into the lantern here.
But do not fret - all is not lost
(Except your figure, at some cost!)."

I then prescribed a tough regime
Of exercise and fruit (no cream),
And steamy baths in natural spas
And scrubbing his particulars.

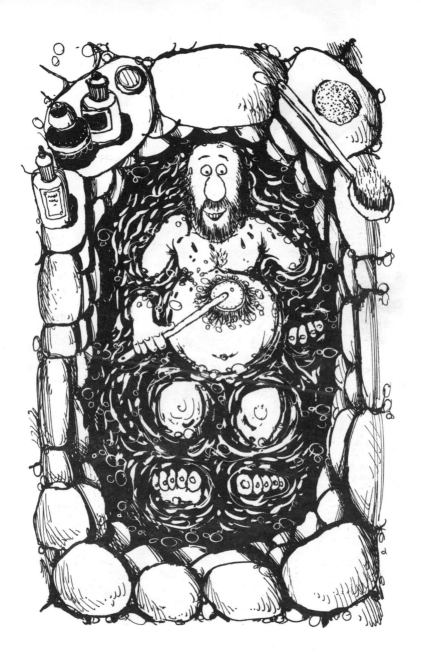

I gave him syrup made of figs
And beat him black and blue with twigs.
I made him walk upon hot coals
Until his socks were full of holes.

He did not like it, not a bit!
And yet I had to make him fit.
I made him sleep on rocky ledges
And I hurled him into hedges.

"Please!" he gasped, "I need to rest!"
"No, No!" I said, "I'm not impressed.
Your jogging vest is still too tight,
Your thighs have dreadful cellulite."

I made him jog to Katmandu,
Then row a single-man canoe
Along the Amazon and back
(No chips, no pizza, no Big Mac).

When he returned, he'd lost a ton.
I never said how well he'd done.
It would have foiled my master plan
Which was to irritate the man.

That may sound very cruel to some
To whom true wisdom doesn't come.
But there was method in my scheme -
Mysterious as that may seem.

I made him suffer day and night
To put his strange condition right,
Until (just as I knew he'd say)
He yelled, "I wish you'd go away!"

It worked! The genie disappeared
Into his lamp. His goatee beard
Went down the spout. He was so slim
At last the lantern fitted him!

He wished me here forever more.
It's rocky and my bum gets sore.
And that is why (or so it's said)
A Yogi stands upon his head!

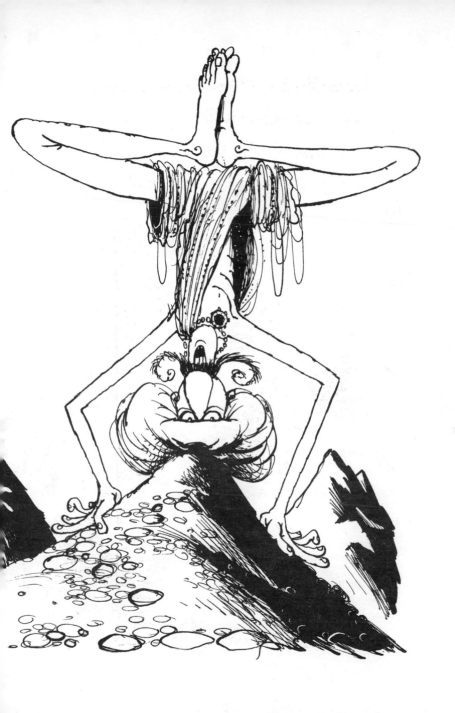

Written by Jeanne Willis * Illustrated by Korky Paul

Jeff the Witch's Chef   1 84362 146 0

Lillibet the Monster Vet   1 84362 145 2

Norman the Demon Doorman   1 84362 159 2

Vanessa the Werewolf Hairdresser   1 84362 148 7

Annie the Gorilla Nanny   1 84362 155 X

Gabby the Vampire Cabbie   1 84362 158 4

Bert the Fairies' Fashion Expert   1 84362 149 5

Iddy Bogey, the Ogre Yogi   1 84362 160 6

All priced at £3.99 each

Crazy Jobs are available from all good book shops, or can be ordered direct
from the publisher: Orchard Books, PO BOX 29, Douglas IM99 1BQ
Credit card orders please telephone 01624 836000
or fax 01624 837033 or visit our Internet site: www.wattspub.co.uk
or e-mail: bookshop@enterprise.net for details.

To order please quote title, author and ISBN
and your full name and address.
Cheques and postal orders should be made payable to 'Bookpost plc.'
Postage and packing is FREE within the UK
(overseas customers should add £1.00 per book).
Prices and availability are subject to change.